Hip, Hip...
Beret!

written by
MELANIE
ELLSWORTH

illustrated by
MORENA
FORZA

HOUGHTON MIFFLIN HARCOURT
BOSTON   NEW YORK

Bella unwraps a beautiful beret—from Grand-père!

Hip, hip . . . Hooray!

But . . . the wind whirls it on its way.

It lands on a horse.
"How dapper!"

Hip, hip . . .
Neigh! Neigh!

"But it doesn't keep the flies at bay."

With a buck, the horse hoofs it on its way.

It lands on a flamenco dancer.
"How charming!"

Hip, hip . . .
Olé!

"But when I dance,
off it floats!"

With a sashay,
she swirls and twirls
it on its way.

It lands on the head of a gentleman.
"How flattering!"

Hip, hip . . .
Toupee!

"But it's rather tight."
With a flick, he flings it
on its way.

It lands in the pan of a famous chef.
"How scrumptious!"

Hip, hip . . .
Soufflé!

"But too chewy!"
With a whisk, she whips
it on its way.

It lands on a
pirouetting child.
"How graceful!"

Hip, hip . . .

It lands on a balloon floating higher and higher.
How uplifting!

Hip, hip . . .
Away!

But . . .

POP!

With a puff, the balloon blows it on its way.

It lands on a skunk.
"How scary!"

Hip, hip . . .
"I'll spray!"

Oh, the poor beret.

There the beret stays,
under sleet and snow
and gray.

Then, one springy, snow-melt day,
up sprouts that beret!

A familiar girl runs out to play.
"No way!"

Hip, hip . . .

Beret!